P9-DNT-902

MAR   2013

for
h, i and j

Published in 2013 by Simply Read Books
www.simplyreadbooks.com
Text & illustrations © 2013 Julie Morstad

Library and Archives Canada Cataloguing in Publication

Morstad, Julie
How to / written and illustrated by Julie Morstad.
ISBN 978-1-897476-57-4
Title.
PS8626.O777H68 2012   jC813'.6   C2010-905676-0

We gratefully acknowledge for their financial support of our publishing
program the Canada Council for the Arts, the BC Arts Council, and the
Government of Canada through the Canada Book Fund (CBF).

Manufactured in Malaysia

Book design by Robin Mitchell Cranfield for hundreds & thousands

10 9 8 7 6 5 4 3 2 1

how to

Julie Morstad

SIMPLY READ BOOKS

how to go fast

how to
go slow

how
to
see
the
wind

how to
feel the breeze

how to be a mermaid

how to have a good sleep

how to make some music

how to make a sandwich

how to make new friends

how to wash
your face

how to wash
your socks

how to how to watch
where you're going

how to
stay close

how to disappear